HarperCollins®, ☎®, HarperFestival®, and Festival Readers™
are trademarks of HarperCollins Publishers, Inc.

Harold and the Purple Crayon: Race Car
Text copyright © 2003 by Adelaide Productions, Inc.
Illustrations copyright © 2003 by Adelaide Productions, Inc.
Printed in the U.S.A. All rights reserved.
Library of Congress catalog card number: 2002110121
www.harperchildrens.com

1 2 3 4 5 6 7 8 9 10

First Edition

HAROLD and the PURPLE CRAYON™

Race Car

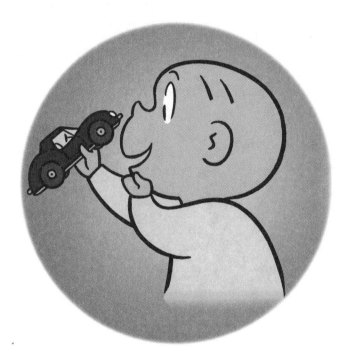

Text by Liza Baker
Illustrations by Kevin Murawski

HarperFestival®
A Division of HarperCollins*Publishers*

It was time for bed,

but Harold was not sleepy.

So he decided to play
with his toy race cars.
Zoom! Zoom!

Toy cars are fun, thought Harold, but imagine how fast I could go in a real race car!

Harold picked up his purple crayon,
drew a road, and set off on an
adventure.

Harold needed a fast car.

So he drew a shiny convertible.

It was just the right size.

He drew racing stripes along the sides.

Then Harold drew

two helmets—

one for him and one for Lilac.

They were ready!

To have a real race,

he needed someone to race against.

So Harold drew another car

and a starting line.

Harold revved his engine.

Three . . . two . . . one . . . GO!

The race had begun!

Harold started out in the lead
but the other car sped past him.
Harold wasn't worried.
He knew he'd catch up.

Soon the road changed.

Harold and Lilac

traveled up a steep hill.

Suddenly Harold

could no longer see the road.

He turned to tell Lilac

but he couldn't see her either.

They were surrounded by fog.

So Harold drew a fan

on the front of his car

to blow away the fog.

Whew!

The road was clear.

The fog was gone.

Once again, they were

on their way.

Up, up, up they went.

Now the road was covered with snow.

Harold's car stopped.

They were stuck in a snowbank.

Thinking quickly,

Harold drew skis for his car.

All around them the snow melted.
Harold and Lilac found themselves
surrounded by sand dunes.

Harold replaced the skis
with huge desert tires.
Off they sped.

Now out of the desert,
they passed hundreds of trees
covered with yellow fruit.
Lemons!

They spotted a farmer surrounded

by bushels of lemons.

He looked like he needed help.

Harold drew a bulldozer bucket

on the front of his car.

He filled it with lemons,

and delivered the load to the barn.

The farmer was thankful.

He offered Harold

a tall glass of lemonade

and a bowl of water to Lilac.

Now it was time

to get back in the race!

Speeding off, they saw the other

race car on the side of the road.

It had broken down.

Harold knew just what to do.

He drew a hitch on his back

bumper and attached the

other car.

Soon they were speeding across
the finish line.

Together!

Harold's racing adventure was fun,

but he was tired and ready to go home.

Harold saw the moon shining above him.

He took his purple crayon
and drew a window around it.

Back in his bedroom,

Harold pulled up his covers.

His purple crayon and toy

race car fell to the floor,

and Harold fell fast asleep.